W9-DFW-444

CELEBRITY BIOS

James Van Der Beek

Kristin McCracken

HIGH
interest
books

Children's Press
A Division of Scholastic Inc.
New York / Toronto / London / Auckland / Sydney
Mexico City / New Delhi / Hong Kong
Danbury, Connecticut

For Trey, Jay and the rest of the Morris clan, with love

Book Design: Michael DeLisio
Contributing Editor: Matthew Pitt

Photo Credits: Cover © Reuters NewMedia, Inc./Corbis; pp. 4, 8, 12, 18, 21, 22, 25, 30, 37 © The Everett Collection; pp. 7, 11, 14, 17, 28, 33 © Retna Ltd.; p. 34 © Nader Group International-Randy Nader/Corbis; p. 38 © AP/Wide World Photos

Visit Children's Press on the Internet at:
http://publishing.grolier.com

Library of Congress Cataloging-in-Publication Data

McCracken, Kristin.
James Van Der Beek / Kristin McCracken.
p. cm. -- (Celebrity bios)
Includes index.
ISBN 0-516-23429-3 (lib. bdg.) -- ISBN 0-516-29604-3 (pbk.)
1. Van Der Beek, James, 1977---Juvenile literature. 2. Actors--United States--Biography--Juvenile literature. I. Title. II. Series.

PN2287.V325 M38 2001
791.45'028'092—dc21
[B]

00-066046

CONTENTS

CHAPTER ONE

Collision Course with Fame

"I played football and I sang. It wasn't quite a match made in heaven...That's why I laugh, because 'Dawson's Creek' has all these female fans, and I was, like, a dork in high school and nobody had a crush on me."
—James on E! Online

Believe it or not, "Dawson's Creek" fans can thank a wild football pass for bringing them James Van Der Beek. While playing junior high school football, the future Dawson Leery was forced out of the game with a concussion. A

James Van Der Beek tried athletics before acting. However, an injury cut his football career short.

football banged the thirteen-year-old on the head, knocking him silly. With his season over, James looked elsewhere for things to do. The local theater was holding auditions, or tryouts. James gave it a shot. In his first audition ever, James landed the lead in the musical *Grease*.

Soon, James had dyed black hair for his role as greaser Danny Zuko. He told *BPI Entertainment News*, "I was looking forward to every performance more than I was looking forward to Christmas."

Without that runaway football, the world might never have discovered James Van Der Beek. The tall, blond charmer might still be playing football somewhere instead of acting.

ALL-AMERICAN FAMILY

Cheshire, Connecticut is a sleepy town where people know their neighbors. In the mid-1970s, Jim and Melinda Van Der Beek were

ready to start a family. James was born on March 8, 1977. He was the couple's first child. A brother, Jared, and a sister, Juliana, followed. The Van Der Beek siblings never fought much. All three children are close.

James inherited talent from both his parents. From his mother, he learned to love performing. Melinda was once a dancer on Broadway.

James's first acting role was in the musical *Grease*.

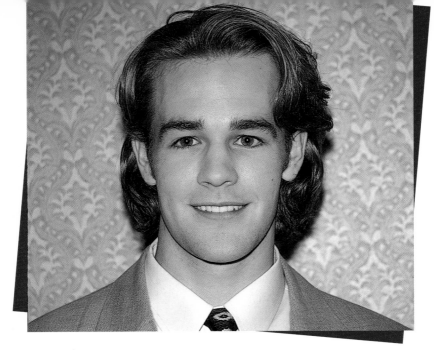
James was a grade "A" student. He earned a scholarship to attend a private school.

James recalled his debut for *Interview* magazine: "I remember being onstage for a recital when I was six, so performing wasn't anything foreign to me when I started doing theater."

James was also no slouch as an athlete. James's father had once played baseball for the Los Angeles Dodgers. It was only natural that his son try baseball, too. Like his father, James had a good arm. James's father was his Little League coach.

LEARNING TO COPE

Soon after James began school, his teachers realized that he was having trouble reading. He was diagnosed with dyslexia. Dyslexia is a condition that can make reading and spelling difficult. No one knows what causes dyslexia. However, teachers can help students overcome it and become successful. James learned to read in a special class and soon rejoined his classmates.

He later earned a scholarship to attend Cheshire Academy, a private school. James was doing it all. He was an honors student, an athlete, and a singer in the school choir.

THE ACTING BUG BITES

In eighth grade, James was playing football on that fateful day. Then that concussion made him take a chance on acting.

Over the years, James built up his acting experience. At age fifteen, he convinced his mother to take him to New York City. Their first stop was a talent agency. James sang his way into a contract with an agent on the very first day! For the next year and a half, James went to auditions whenever he could. He came to know New York City inside and out.

Starting Small

James didn't expect to become a star overnight. He realized that a new face was nothing special. He would have to work hard to get noticed.

James soon got his first role in a TV series. He played Paulie on "Clarissa Explains It All." A young actress named Melissa Joan Hart played the title character. Later, Melissa would become even more

Fun Fact
For much of high school, James served as vice president of his class.

James loves to use his wonderful singing voice whenever he can.

famous, starring in "Sabrina, the Teenage Witch." Though James was only in one episode, his TV experience was far from over.

On a Roll

At seventeen, James worked with the famous playwright Edward Albee. Albee is best known for his play *Who's Afraid of Virginia Woolf?*

James is a sweet guy, yet he was cast as a bully in his first film.

Albee sensed James's talent right away. Albee cast James in his new play, *Finding the Sun*. Later that spring, James was cast in a musical called *Shenandoah*. The play was set in the 1860s. It dealt with fathers and sons going off to war.

CALIFORNIA DREAMIN'

Before James's senior year, the Van Der Beek family took a long vacation in California. While there, James auditioned for movie roles. Almost immediately, he was cast as the bully Rick Sandford in the film *Angus*. In an interview with *Teen People*, James called Rick "the kind of guy who would have beat up Dawson!" Instead of returning to Cheshire Academy, James spent the fall in Minnesota on the set of *Angus*.

Excitement soon turned to disappointment, however. Much of James's performance was cut out of the film. This was quite a blow. James had been sure that *Angus* would be his big break. Instead, critics didn't take much notice.

James's next movie, *I Love You, I Love You Not*, paired him with Claire Danes. Claire would soon become famous for her role with Leonardo DiCaprio in *Romeo + Juliet*. At the time, she was best known as the TV star of "My So-Called Life." In *I Love You, I Love You Not*, James played Tony, another not-so-nice guy. The film finally was released on Halloween in 1997—

almost two years after filming! *I Love You, I Love You Not* wasn't a success. Poor reviews soon landed the film on video store shelves.

THE OLD COLLEGE TRY

James still hadn't found the break he was looking for in the movies. So he decided to give college a chance. James studied at Drew University in New Jersey. Since the school was close to New York City, James also continued his auditions.

After studying English for a year, James was discouraged. He made the dean's list, but schoolwork was not giving him the same charge as acting. Acting jobs also were harder and harder to get. James packed his bags and headed to Europe for a much-needed break. When he returned home, he'd get another break—one that would change his life!

When James returned from a trip to Europe, he had a big surprise waiting for him.

CHAPTER TWO

Awesome Dawson

"I was unemployed and depressed. So I...went backpacking in Europe for six weeks. When I came back, I got a movie, a play, and 'Dawson's Creek'... All of a sudden, everything's different."
—James in US magazine

CREEK AROUND THE CORNER

The WB network was looking for a new drama about teens. Producers discovered a script by the writer Kevin Williamson. Kevin was the creator of the *Scream* movies. He based "Dawson's Creek" on his own experiences as a teenager.

The WB network had high hopes that James would become one of its first big stars.

Although it was nerve-wracking, James's audition for "Dawson's Creek" was a huge success!

This new show was not about spoiled kids living in Beverly Hills or smart-aleck sons of single moms. It was a show about young adults struggling with the real issues facing today's teenagers. The WB's executives decided to take a risk. Now they needed to find their Dawson.

Perfect Fit

James auditioned for the role of fifteen-year-old Dawson in the spring of 1997. He had just turned twenty. "He was really nervous, and it showed," Kevin told *People*. Yet James came back for a second reading "and stunned us. We knew he was Dawson. He's very bright, but he's also very vulnerable."

The producers had found their lead. The show was set to start. Ads promoting the show popped up everywhere, before it even began. James and his co-stars (Joshua Jackson, Katie Holmes, and Michelle Williams) were even featured in a J. Crew catalog. However, James's face was front and center. He was clearly the star.

START OF SOMETHING BIG

"Dawson's Creek" premiered in January 1998. Audiences across the nation began tuning in. Finally, there was a show that didn't assume teenagers were interested only in shopping and proms. Kevin Williamson explained the show's appeal to *Starweek* magazine. "I do sort of feel like teenagers in general are underestimated," he said. "I felt underestimated when I was that age. I thought I was capable of so much more...than adults gave me credit for."

As every fan knows, Dawson Leery is an only child. He's obsessed with talking, films, and his beautiful pal (and occasional girlfriend),

Fun Fact

James's first paying job was acting in an acne commercial. His face was supposed to be clear. However, on the morning of the shoot, James discovered that he'd broken out overnight! Luckily, the makeup people were able to cover up his pimples.

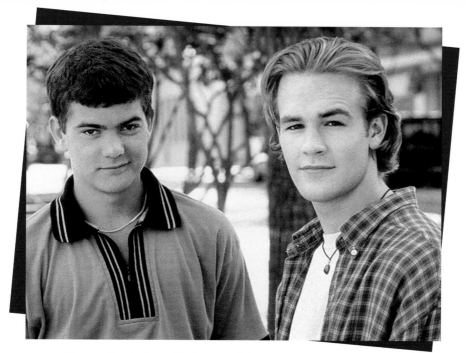

For a short time, Joshua and James were roommates.

Joey Potter. He lives in the fictional town of Capeside, Massachusetts. Dawson's a nice guy, but he has his wild side, too.

James likes the way the show is written. He's happy that audiences can relate to Dawson and his friends. He explained to *E! Online*, "I like the fact that all the characters are honest, yet flawed in some ways. I mean, the dialogue is great, but even more than that, what's going on underneath it is really incredible."

Sparks often fly between Joey and Dawson. In real life, however, James and Katie are just good friends.

THE SET

The young stars work hard. Sometimes their work days last 18 hours! It certainly helps that they're all good friends. They enjoy the Wilmington nightlife. The townspeople have gotten used to their famous neighbors. James laughingly told *Seventeen*, "The locals in

Wilmington are probably sick of me getting up and singing [karaoke]."

James's co-stars think highly of him. "James is very graceful," Michelle told *People*. "A very smooth, even, cool guy." Michelle plays Dawson's former love interest Jen.

Katie agreed completely in *Seventeen*. "He's kind of quiet, very conservative but very sweet. We're like brother and sister."

When they first moved to Wilmington, James and Joshua (who plays pal Pacey Witter) shared an apartment. James was neat and organized. Joshua was the total opposite. The cast and crew started calling them "The Odd Couple."

THE FAME GAME

The show was a hit. James's fame skyrocketed too. On *E! Online*, he recalled a trip to meet fans in Seattle, Washington. "I had no idea that 5,000 screaming teenagers would come. I just didn't know what to do...The security guards had to whisk me offstage, and they sent the limo off empty because people were swarming it. They took me out in a police car."

This was only the beginning. Within a year of Dawson's debut, James had a starring role in a major motion picture. This time, his part wasn't cut out! He played Jonathan "Mox" Moxon in *Varsity Blues*. Moxon is a second-string high school quarterback who becomes a Texas-sized hero. Veteran actor Jon Voight played Mox's coach. Voight impressed James and taught him some acting tips. "He was just so helpful, so generous, and I learned a huge amount," James told *Teen Tribute*. "That was the highlight of the film for me."

Varsity Blues—starring James with a Southern drawl—was a box-office smash. It was the most popular movie in the United States for

In *Varsity Blues,* James worked with legendary actor Jon Voight. James describes the time as a great learning experience.

three weeks! The movie also had rising stars Paul Walker and Scott Caan. Plus, it featured real high school football players from Texas.

In an interview with The WB, James explained what it was like playing a character so different from Dawson. "[Mox] would never hang out with Dawson. The two would never be seen in the same social circles. [Mox] is very aggressive, he's an athlete, basically everything Dawson is not. It was fun to get to expand and play somebody different."

James also was able to use his athletic ability, which he doesn't get to do on "Dawson's Creek." To prepare for the role, James practiced his football skills. He tried not to think about the ball that knocked him out in junior high. James had three weeks to train. By the time filming began, he was making great passes.

Fun Fact

In *Varsity Blues*, it's no accident that Mox wears the number four on his jersey. Number four is also the number on the jersey of Brett Favre of the Green Bay Packers. Brett is James's favorite quarterback!

For James, playing Mox was also a career move. He told *Teen People,* "Hopefully, people will see me as an actor as opposed to just a television personality. But I can't stay up worrying what other people are going to think of me."

POKING FUN

In 1999, James also got to host "Saturday Night Live." James and the cast performed many skits. A few of them involved the "Dawson's Creek" cast. James showed that he could make fun of himself. He was not arrogant, or too proud of his success.

The 2000 film *Scary Movie* spoofed, or made fun of, recent teen horror films. These films included *Scream* and *I Know What You Did Last Summer.* James had a small role in *Scary Movie* as a character named "Dawson Lerry." Young audiences roared with laughter from coast to coast.

CHAPTER THREE

Life as a Star

"Dawson...[is] a bit of an innocent, and is frequently off in his own little world, all of which I can definitely relate to."
—James in TV Guide

Being a young star means being a role model for teens everywhere. Kids look to their favorite celebrities for advice on fashion, dating, and grooming. James lets his TV character give most of the advice. However, he does have a few secrets to share.

James enjoys dressing up for a night on the town.

James doesn't have to put much effort into looking good.

BEAUTY SECRETS

Like Dawson, James prefers comfortable clothes. His relaxed style, including khakis and untucked, button-down shirts, dates back to his days at Cheshire Academy. James was a good student. He was able to break some of the school's dress-code rules, such as wearing a blazer.

Nights out are a different story. At a movie premiere or a network event, James often wears a stylish suit and tie.

Playing a teenager every week can be difficult for a man in his early twenties. As he told *People*, "For 'Dawson's Creek,' I have to shave a lot. I shave twice every day." Other than lots of shaving cream, the star doesn't use any special beauty products. "Soap is good," he explains.

Some actors work for hours to have a natural look. James's carefree routine doesn't take any time at all. Even his blond hair behaves without any effort. "I basically jump in the shower, throw a hat on and take it off at work. In half an hour, my hair is cool...I wear it both ways, but on formal occasions, brim forward."

FRIENDS AND ROMANCE

The teen years are never easy, not even for James. Just like Dawson, he didn't always get the girl. True friends also were hard to find. He told *TV Guide*, "I think everyone remembers those miserable school dances where you're just walking around trying to look like you had somebody to be with... getting a tray in the cafeteria and having no one to sit with... I'm sure you remember that first girlfriend who dumped you, the one who broke your heart. Those are things that stay with you. No matter what you've experienced or how much you've grown."

Making friends is both easier and harder for James now that he's famous. Sometimes it's hard to know whom he can trust. Some people may be true friends. Others may be attracted only to his money and star status. "It's not necessarily a bad thing, it's just a matter of getting comfortable with [it]," James told *TV Guide*. "It's kind of strange. You haven't changed at all, it's just that everyone around you treats you differently."

Fun Fact

In college, James was in an *a cappella* singing group called 36 Madison Ave.

Though he loves giving interviews, James prefers to
keep his romantic life private.

James and his co-stars have become good
friends. Part of the reason is that they all deal
with the same fame issues. Romance also has
blossomed for the young star. He's been dating
the same woman for several years. However, he
never talks about her in interviews. He prefers
to keep that side of his life private.

CHAPTER FOUR

What's Next?

"The problem with teen idols is that they grow up. The trick is to prove you're an actor in the process. I'm trying to establish myself as an actor as opposed to a novelty, but I can use the novelty-item status to get opportunities to act."
—*James in* Movieline

THE FUTURE

What does the future hold for James Van Der Beek? We can only guess. One thing is certain. There's no end in sight for "Dawson's Creek." James told *USA Today* that he is still happy on the set. "Being in a television show offers a

James chooses to work through his summer breaks. He uses this time to act in movies.

tremendous amount of security…I'll stay as long as they keep me."

Starring in a TV show also means that the actors get three months off. This vacation period is called a hiatus. This gives the actors time to make movies. James already has starred in one major feature film in 2001. It's the movie *Texas Rangers*, which came out in the spring. In *Texas Rangers*, James plays a cowboy in the Wild West. The other stars included Dylan McDermott and R&B singer Usher. Rachael Leigh Cook (of the hit movie *She's All That*) also starred in the film.

COMING ATTRACTIONS

James also is in a new film by Todd Solondz. Todd is the director of the films *Welcome to the Dollhouse* and *Happiness*. James's character is named Graham. The film is scheduled to debut in 2001. The movie is still untitled.

James recently starred as a cowboy in the film *Texas Rangers*.

James always has been interested in writing. He may decide to become a screenwriter someday. He told *16* magazine, "I write prose and a couple of short plays. I finished a screenplay but it's in no condition to be shot because I don't know everything about the technical side of film. But it's actually a lot of fun to try and write something."

BROADWAY BABY

James has found success on screens both big and small. Yet he's never forgotten his first love, the theater. Fans might be able to catch James on Broadway during his next hiatus.

James Van Der Beek has become America's favorite boy next door. Unlike many other stars, James has made a successful leap from TV to the movies. He's landed at the top of the box office. His good looks and clean-cut image have charmed people of all ages.

James's roller-coaster ride to fame has just begun. This young actor expects to try new and exciting things for many years to come. Millions of fans are very glad that James didn't duck when that football headed his way.

James was overjoyed when he won an MTV Movie Award. His fans expect him to win many more awards in the future.

TIMELINE

1977 • James is born in Cheshire, Connecticut, on March 8.

1993 • James is a guest star on the TV show "Clarissa Explains It All."

1994 • James stars in two plays: *Finding the Sun* and *Shenandoah*.
     • James is cast in his first film, *Angus*.

1995 • James is "Tony" in the film *I Love You, I Love You Not*, released on Halloween in 1997.

1997 • James is cast as Dawson Leery in the TV series "Dawson's Creek."

1998 • "Dawson's Creek" debuts on The WB network on January 22.
     • *People* names James one of their 50 Most Beautiful People.

1999 • James stars as Jonathan "Mox" Moxon in the film *Varsity Blues*, which opens in January.

TIMELINE

1999
- James wins an MTV Movie Award for Best Breakthrough Male Performance for his work in *Varsity Blues*.
- James stars in the film *Harvest*.
- James hosts "Saturday Night Live."

2000
- James has a small part as "Dawson Lerry" in *Scary Movie*.

2001
- The Western *Texas Rangers* is released in the spring.
- James acts in a movie directed by Todd Solondz.

FACT SHEET

Name	James William Van Der Beek, Jr.
Nickname	James Van Der Geek (as a kid)
Born	March 8, 1977
Birthplace	Cheshire, Connecticut
Family	Mother, Melinda; father, Jim; younger brother, Jared; younger sister, Juliana
Hometown	Cheshire, Connecticut
	Lives in Wilmington, North Carolina when filming "Dawson's Creek"
Sign	Pisces
Hair	Blond
Eyes	Brown, with a hint of green
Height	6'

Favorites

Car	Toyota 4Runner
Books	*Portrait of the Artist as a Young Man* by James Joyce; *The Crucible* by Arthur Miller; *The Sound and the Fury* by William Faulkner
Music	James Taylor, Dave Matthews Band, The Beatles, cast recordings from Broadway shows
Hobbies	Singing, playing guitar, writing, and going to the theater
Sports	Baseball, football, swimming—just about everything!

NEW WORDS

agent someone who helps a performer find work

arrogant boastful about your talents

audition a tryout

Broadway street that's home to some of New York City's most popular theaters

critic someone who gives an opinion about a work of art

debut a performer's first appearance

hiatus when a TV show takes a break from filming

role a character or part played by an actor

screenplay the script for a movie

script the lines characters say in a movie, play, or TV show

set the place where a movie or TV show is filmed

sitcom a TV comedy

spoof a film or TV skit that makes fun of a successful show or film

FOR FURTHER READING

Tresniowski, Alex. *Boy Next Door: The James Van Der Beek Story*. New York: Ballantine Books, 1999.

Furman, Leah and Elina Furman. *James Van Der Beek*. New York: St. Martin Paperbacks, 1999.

Catalano, Grace. *Meet the Stars of Dawson's Creek*. New York: Bantam Books, 1998.

Altman, Sheryl and Sheryl Berk. *Way Too Much Information: A Fanatic's Guide to Dawson's Creek*. New York: Harperactive, 1998.

Crosdale, Darren and Patty Rice. *Dawson's Creek: The Official Companion*. Kansas City, MO: Andrews McMeel Publishing, 1999.

RESOURCES

Web Sites
E! Entertainment Television
www.eonline.com
This Web site features bios, photos, and the latest news on all your favorite stars.

Internet Movie Database
www.imdb.com
This site lists acting credits for your favorite celebrities. Check in and learn about James's next acting project!

The Official "Dawson's Creek" Web site
www.dawsonscreek.com
Look here for advance plot information, cast bios, and episode guides.

Varsity Blues
www.varsityblues.com
This is the official Web site for the film. Get the inside scoop on James's first leading role!

RESOURCES

You can write to James at the following address:
James Van Der Beek
c/o "Dawson's Creek"
The WB Network
4000 Warner Boulevard
Burbank, CA 91522

INDEX

INDEX

About the Author

Kristin McCracken is an educator and writer living in New York City. Her favorite activities include seeing movies, plays, and the occasional star on the street.